Born To Howl

More Devilish Fun with C.D. Bitesky, Howie Wolfner, Elisa and Frankie Stein, and Danny Keegan
From Avon Camelot

M IS FOR MONSTER

THERE'S A BATWING IN MY LUNCHBOX
THE PET OF FRANKENSTEIN
Z IS FOR ZOMBIE

Born To Howl

Mel Gilden

Illustrated by John Pierard

A GLC BOOK

AN AVON CAMELOT BOOK

BORN TO HOWL is an original publication of Avon Books. This work has never before appeared in book form.

AVON BOOKS
A division of
The Hearst Corporation
105 Madison Avenue
New York, New York 10016

Developed by Byron Preiss and Dan Weiss
Edited by Ruth Ashby
Front cover painting by Steve Fastner and John Pierard

First Camelot Printing: December 1987

Printed in the U.S.A.

OPM 10 9 8 7 6 5 4

Chapter One

A Foggy Night in Brooklyn

The fog began to roll in while Danny Keegan and his sister, Barbara, were walking home from the library. Side by side they walked across the park while cottony walls thickened and closed in around them. Danny had his arm load of books about European folklore and monster movies, Barbara her books about woodcraft and surviving on roots and berries.

Danny's interest in monsters grew out of his friendship with the new kids in his fifth grade class at P.S. 13, each of whom reminded him of a monster he had seen in movies or read about. All four of them were nice enough, and had even become his best friends, but that didn't keep Danny from noticing their little quirks and oddball characteristics.

Barbara was a year younger than Danny. Danny had never seen her voluntarily read anything before except books about horses. She had developed an interest in staying alive in the wilderness—a skill she would probably not need in Brooklyn—when she joined the Girls' Pathfinders.

Danny walked more slowly. The fog was now so thick that he couldn't see more than half a block away.

He felt as if he were walking through a big room whose walls kept moving so that he was always in the center. Close sounds seemed muffled, while far-off sounds seemed loud and unnaturally clear. At the moment, close sounds consisted mostly of the squeak of their shoes as they walked across the wet grass and of Barbara's voice.

Barbara went on and on about the Girls' Pathfinders. They made crafts and went on cookouts and learned camp songs. Anything Barbara had to say, Danny had heard before. He and his parents had heard little else for weeks. He wasn't really listening. He was thinking.

He was thinking about old black-and-white horror movies, the kind he saw on television. And the longer he and Barbara walked, the more Danny felt that he was inside one of them.

Those movies sometimes started with a couple of comic grave diggers walking across a cemetery in heavy fog. They scared each other with monster stories and with noises they made when they themselves stepped on crackling twigs. Suddenly—always suddenly—they would hear the howling of a wolf far off in the fog. Next thing you knew, one of them was dead under mysterious circumstances and the other one was running for his life. Before long, somebody like Sherlock Holmes or Baron von Frankenstein was usually involved.

And now, here were Barbara and Danny, doing—except for the part about the cemetery—exactly what those two grave diggers were always doing. The thing that gave Danny a creepy feeling was the fact that, except for the gravestones, wasn't a park a lot like a cemetery? And weren't there things—er, people—in Brooklyn that Danny would never have guessed lived there if he hadn't been going to school with them? And if there were friendly monsters in Brooklyn, might there not be monsters who were not so friendly?

Barbara had stopped talking for a moment, probably to breathe, Danny thought. He took this opportunity to say, "Looking at those books, a person would think the Girls' Pathfinders were going to drop you in the middle of a jungle with nothing but a compass and a canteen of water."

Barbara was not amused by Danny's comment. "You haven't been listening to me. The Girls' Pathfinders are going out to Long Island on a cookout on Halloween eve, and I want to be ready for it. Besides, I have to know my woodsy lore if I'm going to get my Girls' Pathfinders merit badge for woodcraft and survival. Can't you walk any faster?"

"What's your hurry?" The fog was getting denser. Danny was slowing down so he wouldn't run into anything.

"Mrs. Bumpo, my Girls' Pathfinders counselor, is coming over tonight with my Big Pal." Ever since Barbara had joined the Girls' Pathfinders, one of the major questions in her life—aside from how to survive in the wilds of Long Island—was who her Big Pal would be.

A Big Pal was a fifth grade girl who would do everything with Barbara, her Little Pal. She would initiate Barbara into the mysteries of girlhood and of Girls' Pathfinderhood. They would be a team and share many secrets. Barbara had wanted Laurie Perry to be her Big

3

Pal. But Mrs. Bumpo had told Barbara that one of the important social skills a Girls' Pathfinder must learn is how to make new friends. That was why only the counselors chose who was to be Pals with whom.

Barbara had heard horrible tales of Big and Little Pals who simply did not get along, ruining everybody's time in the club. She didn't even want to think about the possibility of getting someone she didn't like as a Big Pal. Still, the possibility existed and continued to nibble at the back of Barbara's mind.

Barbara clutched her books more tightly to her chest. "Oh, I hope she's somebody nice. I wouldn't want to be paired off with somebody icky."

"You'd better hope Mrs. Bumpo is pairing you with Davy Crockett if you want to survive on Long Island."

"That shows you what you know. There aren't any boys in the Girls' Pathfinders. Besides, you're just making fun of me. You don't think Long Island is so tough."

"It's not exactly untouched by human hands," Danny said.

"Maybe not," Barbara said, "but that doesn't mean you can't get lost or fall and break your leg or get a snakebite." She thought about what other disaster could befall her. Not one of them seemed awful enough to serve as an example. "Or something," she finally said.

"We could get lost in Brooklyn tonight," Danny said as he peered into the fog.

For the first time, Barbara noticed how the fog was closing in. In the murkiness, the park did not look familiar, though she had been there a thousand times

4

before. Her books said that if you are lost, it's better to wait in one place than to wander around. Well, she wasn't quite lost yet. Besides, it would be very embarrassing if she and Danny had to be rescued in Brooklyn, mere blocks from home.

Suddenly, far away, something howled. Dogs all over the neighborhood began to bark. Danny and Barbara froze in their tracks and tried to see what the fog was hiding. Just like in the old black-and-white movies. Dark shapes, tall gangly trees, and dwarflike bushes loomed out of the fog like monsters.

"What was that?" Barbara said.

"Some dog," Danny said, but he himself was not so sure. He had heard a howl like that before in his classroom at P.S. 13, and it hadn't been a dog.

Whatever it was howled again, this time closer.

"Do something, Danny," Barbara whispered.

Danny was about to remind Barbara that *he* was not the Girls' Pathfinder, when he heard something moving around in the bushes. It was very close, but because of the impenetrable fog, he couldn't even see the bushes, let alone what was hiding in them. Even though he thought he knew what was out there and that there was nothing to fear, his heart beat faster and he wished that he had X-ray vision.

"Hey," said Danny, "it's OK. Just some dog. This isn't Long Island, after all."

"Right. Sure." Barbara's smile lived and died on her face in seconds.

A shape, low and dark as a bush, loped at them out of the murk. Barbara made a little "oh" sound when she saw it, backed off a few steps, then suddenly ran across

5

the wet grass the way she and Danny had come, screaming for help.

"Wait," Danny cried as he ran after her.

Soon Barbara and Danny were running neck and neck, and the thing was gaining on them. "It's just Howie Wolfner," Danny said between gasps.

Barbara didn't have the breath to tell Danny that knowing the thing's name didn't reassure her. This episode was just further proof of how strange Danny's new friends actually were. She wished her mother and father were here to see this. They might not be so quick with their "different is OK" speech.

Howie Wolfner, or whatever it was, ran alongside them. Barbara could see that it was something like a dog but something like a human too. It had pointed ears and a snout like a dog. Hair covered everything. But it ran on its hind legs and knuckles, the way a gorilla might. It howled again, and Barbara shivered with a sudden chill.

The doglike thing ran circles around Barbara and Danny, then suddenly stopped in front of them and stood there panting with its tongue out. Barbara was forced to stop or run into the creature. Danny stopped beside her. Both of them were breathing hard.

"Uh, hi, Howie," Danny said. He was uncertain if Howie would recognize his name when he was in wolf form, but Howie yipped a time or two and trotted over to them. Barbara looked around wildly, obviously ready to cut and run again. Danny took her hand and said, "He won't hurt you," and hoped he was right.

Howie was polite, even in wolf form. Instead of leaping on them as a friendly dog might, he sat down in front of them and looked from one to the other.

"Pet him," Danny said.

"You pet him," Barbara said. "He's your friend."

The logic of this was inescapable. Danny shifted his library books under one arm, and with his free hand gently patted the long, stiff hair on top of Howie's head. "Good Howie. Good Howie," Danny said, feeling very silly. After all, he would not have done this if Howie were in his human form.

Far away, something howled. Howie looked up suddenly, and Danny pulled his hand back.

"Another one?" Barbara said.

"Family," Danny guessed. He'd never met Howie's parents, but there was no reason why he shouldn't have a set just like everybody else.

Something flapped by above them. "That's not a bird," Barbara cried. She was evidently correct because a big thing that sounded like someone quickly opening and closing a leather wallet flew over their heads and landed on the grass next to Howie. "It's a bat!" Barbara shrieked and ran. Howie was as surprised by the bat's arrival as Barbara, and he ran off in the direction from which the howl came.

Danny looked down at the bat and said, "How you doing, C.D.?" The bat opened its mouth and screeched in a way that rapidly rose too high for Danny to hear.

In the distance something howled again, and a moment later something else answered it. Whether the howling came from the throats of dogs or werewolves, Danny did not know. But he had his suspicions. No dog howl had ever raised the tiny hairs on the back of Danny's neck the way these did.

The bat leaped into the air and flapped off on busi-

ness of its own. Danny stood on the grassy field for a moment, watching it disappear into a swirl of fog. It occurred to him that he was alone. Despite himself, he became frightened of things he imagined might still be hidden in the white walls of cloud.

This time Barbara had run in the direction of home. Hefting his books under his other arm, Danny followed her as quickly as he could.

Barbara did not stop running until she reached her front door. She dropped her survival books and fished into her tiny red plastic purse for her house key. She found it, but it fell onto the step twice before she got it into the keyhole. She jiggled the key, looking over her shoulder again and again, expecting at any moment to see the army of monsters she was certain was chasing her.

She got the door open at last and, after picking up the books, heaved herself into the house, slammed the door, and stood there breathing hard. She pondered whether it was worthwhile to cry. It occurred to her that Girls' Pathfinders probably did not cry. But she did allow her lip to tremble.

"Is that you?" Mrs. Keegan called from the living room.

"Yes, Mom," Barbara called as she walked into the living room, "and you should be glad I'm still alive." Barbara was about to continue her story when she saw who was sitting with her mother eating sandwich cookies from the good china. She stopped short, horrified.

"Where's Danny?" Mrs. Keegan said, as if Barbara had not just had a very big shock in an evening that seemed full of big shocks.

"He'll be here soon," Barbara said. She was going to add, *If the monsters didn't get him,* but even though she was scared, her company manners slid into gear and stopped her.

Mrs. Keegan said, "You know Mrs. Bumpo, don't you, Barbara?"

Not trusting herself to speak, Barbara nodded politely to Mrs. Bumpo.

Mrs. Bumpo was a plump, serious woman who smiled frequently. But no smile lasted long, seeming to die from lack of interest. She was wearing practical shoes and her Girls' Pathfinders uniform—a simple brown dress with insignia on the arms. Her substantial chest was covered with medals, ribbons, and merit badges. Mrs. Bumpo had been in the Girls' Pathfinders for a long time, since she had been a little girl. Even though, or perhaps because, she had no children of her own, she had stayed in it and become a counselor long after most girls had lost interest.

Mrs. Bumpo stood up and removed her glasses from where they pinched the bridge of her nose. This was easy because the glasses had no earpieces. With the glasses, she indicated the girl sitting in the wing-backed chair next to the couch. "I'm sure you know Elisa Stein," she said. "She is to be your Big Pal."

Elisa said, "I am looking forward to being Pals, Barbara."

Without enthusiasm, Barbara said, "Sure."

It was very quiet in the room. Someone ran up the steps outside, dropped something that could have been a pile of books, and jingled a key into the lock. Nobody said anything as Danny rushed into the house and slammed the door behind him. He walked into the room, his face flushed, and said, "Hi, Mom." He saw the look on Barbara's face and then noticed Elisa Stein, half a cookie held delicately in one hand.

"Hello, Danny," Elisa said.

"Hi, Elisa." He looked at his mom. "Uh, anything wrong?"

"I think," Mrs. Keegan said carefully, "that your sister is overwhelmed at the prospect of Elisa being her Big Pal."

"Overwhelmed!" Barbara cried. "Monsters everywhere! I can't get away from them! Look at the bumps on her neck! She's some kind of thing from a horror movie!" Barbara ran from the room and up the stairs, crying hysterically.

Mrs. Keegan said, "I must apologize for Barbara. Did something happen on the way home, Danny?"

"We sort of ran into Howie and C.D.," Danny said.

"Why should that—?"

Elisa interrupted Mrs. Keegan by saying, "It is fine, Mrs. Keegan. Do not trouble yourself. I understand."

"That's very good of you, Elisa," said Mrs. Bumpo. "But I'm afraid that Barbara will have to change her unfortunate attitude if she is to remain a Girls' Pathfinder."

"I am sure," said Elisa, "that we will be good friends by the end of the month, when it is time for the Pathfinders cookout."

"I'm sure you're right, Elisa," Mrs. Keegan said. She glanced at the staircase. "Danny, would you please see Elisa and Mrs. Bumpo to the door? I'm going upstairs to talk to your sister."

11

Things would probably go badly for Barbara, Danny thought. They always went badly when one of his parents referred to their child by relationship instead of by name.

It didn't matter what his mother said to Barbara. Danny was familiar with Barbara's attitude toward his monster friends, and he didn't think that a parental lecture or hanging around with Elisa would be enough to change it.

From everything he'd seen and heard, prejudice was a pretty tough number. Unless something spectacular happened, Barbara would stay upset about Elisa being her Big Pal. She might even drop out of the Girls' Pathfinders. And, Danny thought, she would probably blame it on poor Elisa.

Mrs. Keegan ran up the stairs while Danny said, "So, how you doing, Elisa?"

"Your sister seems very upset."

"Yeah, well, she's kind of high-strung."

"I was a very high-strung child myself," Mrs. Bumpo said, "but that's no reason for this outburst." She slipped her glasses back on her nose and strode toward the front door as if she were leading a parade. Danny and Elisa followed her.

"It'll be fun tomorrow at the wax museum," Danny said to Elisa.

"Fun, yes. Ms. Cosgrove has many interesting educational ideas."

Interesting was certainly the word for Ms. Cosgrove, their fifth grade teacher. She was enthusiastic about everything. The girls adored her, and the boys were in love with her. If Danny hadn't been in love with her

12

himself, he would have thought the whole situation was pretty disgusting.

Danny said goodby to Elisa and Mrs. Bumpo and closed the door. He looked at the staircase and wondered how his mother was doing.

When Mrs. Keegan came in carrying a glass of water, Barbara was facedown on her pink chenille bedspread, crying. Mrs. Keegan sat down on the bed and offered her the glass of water. Still sniffling, Barbara sat up and drank the water in small sips. There was space between her and her mother on the bed.

After a while, Mrs. Keegan said, "What was that all about?"

Barbara spoke again about monsters. She didn't like to watch the dumb old movies that Danny watched, but she had seen parts of them by mistake while walking through the room, so she knew about them. Once, Danny had convinced her to watch *Dracula* all the way through. The movie was old and the sound track hissed during the long parts where nobody said much of anything. The guy who played the vampire had so much grease on his hair it looked as if it were a solid piece of plastic. The movie was icky, but it wasn't scary.

Still, you had to be careful. People who sucked your blood or removed your brain or attacked you like a wild animal obviously could not be trusted. Barbara tried to explain this to her mother.

"Elisa is a perfectly normal girl," Mrs. Keegan said.

"Didn't you see those lumps on her neck?"

"Lots of people have skin problems."

"You just don't want to understand!" Barbara wailed.

She began to cry again, though she was certain it would not do any good. The fact that it would do no good was one of the reasons she cried.

Mrs. Keegan smoothed Barbara's hair and said, "There, there." Eventually, Barbara stopped crying again. She sat up and had some more water and sniffled. She and her mother talked some more about monsters—what they were like and why she thought Elisa was one. Mrs. Keegan nodded, but not with great sincerity, Barbara thought.

"What about the Girls' Pathfinders?" Mrs. Keegan said.

"Yeah," Barbara said, wondering about them. All the girls in her glass were members. If she let Elisa Stein make her quit, she would be a social outcast. At last she sighed and said, "Will you talk to Mrs. Bumpo?"

"If you want me to. But I think you should be prepared to make the best of this. Mrs. Bumpo does not strike me as the kind of woman who changes her mind easily."

"Yeah," Barbara said.

"Meanwhile," Mrs. Keegan said with finality, "you try to be the best Little Pal you can be to Elisa Stein."

"I'll try," Barbara said. "But if your own daughter comes home one day without a brain, don't say I didn't warn you."

Chapter Two

The Werewolf Strikes

It's definitely getting colder, Danny thought. Wind seemed to whip right through him. Next to him, Barbara walked sullenly, head down, deep in thought. She clutched a book called *The Big Book of Woodlore* to her chest.

"So," said Danny, "how's fourth grade?"

"OK," said Barbara.

Danny waited for her to say more, but she didn't. He knew what she was thinking about. She was thinking about Elisa Stein. Nothing else could be making her so gloomy.

"So," said Danny, "are you about ready to brave Long Island?"

"I don't want to talk about it."

"Not talk about it? That's all you've been talking about for weeks."

Barbara nodded and sniffled. Maybe it was just a cold coming on. Maybe not.

Barbara was Danny's little sister. She looked up to him, and he was a lot closer to her age than their mom was. Maybe he could get through to her. He said, "Look, Elisa's not so bad."

"That's what you say. She's probably removed *your* brain already. Maybe that's why you're her friend."

"What would she do with my brain? Or with *yours* either, for that matter?"

"I don't know. I'm not some kind of Frankenstein."

"Frankenstein was the scientist. Not the monster."

"I'm not either one, so what does it matter? If you want to know what Elisa Stein wants to do with my brain, then ask *her*. She's *your* friend."

Despite the tone of the conversation, Danny was encouraged by the fact that Barbara was talking at all. He said, "So, are you going to the Girls' Pathfinders meeting after school, or what?"

"None of your beeswax."

"Elisa's OK. Trust me."

They talked around in circles all the way to school but neither of them made any progress changing the other's point of view. Still, Barbara thought that she might go to the Girls' Pathfinders meeting after all. She wasn't ready yet to take the final step and drop out. And if she wasn't dropping out, she would have to go to the meeting. Maybe if her mom talked to Mrs. Bumpo, Mrs. Bumpo would let her be Laurie Perry's Little Pal. Even if not, what could Elisa do to her at school with all that adult supervision around?

Just before she ran off to Mrs. Sears's fourth grade room, Barbara said, "You tell Elisa Stein that I have the police and the F.B.I. watching her. She'd better not try anything funny."

On the bus to the Price Wax Museum, Stevie Brickwald threw things out the window whenever he thought Ms.

16

Cosgrove wasn't watching. She caught him a time or two, and at last made him sit next to her. Danny wasn't sure, but sitting next to Ms. Cosgrove may have been what Stevie had in mind all along. Ms. Cosgrove was an odd teacher. She inspired that kind of soppy behavior in students who were usually pretty normal.

Danny sat next to Elisa Stein. Across the aisle was Howie Wolfner, now in the form of a fifth grade boy who had a really extraordinary mane of reddish brown hair. In front of Danny was Elisa's twin brother, Frankie. He was a lot bigger than any other kid on the bus, almost as tall as Ms. Cosgrove. He had knobs on his neck, just the way Elisa did. Ms. Cosgrove thought the knobs had something to do with braces they had to wear after a bad traffic accident. It was amazing what some adults would believe.

Next to Frankie was C.D. Bitesky. He was not a bat at the moment. The top of his head barely rose above the back of the seat. His well-kept black hair shone in the bright sunlight.

When the bus pulled up in front of the Price Wax Museum, Ms. Cosgrove stood up next to the driver, faced her students, and said, "This is the big moment, kids! But don't forget that we're not here at the wax museum just to have a good time. This is part of our unit on religion and superstition. Pay particular attention to the Chamber of Horrors. That's where you'll see representations of the strange kinds of stuff people used to believe in. Even today, some folks have really bizarre ideas about who and what make the world go round. OK! Let's hit it!"

Ms. Cosgrove pointed to the bus driver. He pushed a

button, and the door hissed as it opened. With a forward-ho motion, Ms. Cosgrove turned and walked down the steps. When she turned, her long blond hair fanned out for a moment.

Everybody began to talk and laugh. Danny saw Jason Nickles rub his hands together like an old man and cackle like a witch for the benefit of Stevie Brickwald. With one hand, Stevie pulled his jacket up and over his nose as if it were a cape and peered over the top of it. He laughed like a maniac.

Danny edged his way up the aisle behind Elisa Stein. Howie Wolfner looked back at them and said, "This may be a difficult adventure for all of us. May I walk with you?"

Elisa said that she would be delighted. C.D., who wore a real cape over his formal clothes all the time, let the straw drop from his mouth back into the Thermos bottle that held what he called his Fluid of Life. The Fluid was mysterious red stuff that he had gotten permission to drink, even during class. Nobody knew what was in the Fluid. Danny had a theory, but he was not in a hurry to find out if it was correct.

Speaking with an exotic East European accent, C.D. said, "As Howie suggests, perhaps we Children of the Night will be more comfortable if we all stay together." He dropped his Thermos bottle into a pocket sewn into the red lining of his cape.

"And Danny, of course," said Frankie.

As they moved up the aisle to the door, Elisa spoke to Danny. She said, "Despite Howie's fears, I do not expect the Chamber of Horrors to tell us anything we do not already know. Years ago, in the Old Country, people were especially fearful of anyone who was not like themselves. Unusual people were hunted down and their ends were, more often than not, unpleasant. Today we are more relaxed.''

"Halloween is coming," Howie grumbled.

"That is true," Elisa said. "But Halloween is not the difficult time for us that it once was. As I said, today we are more relaxed. Do you not find it so, Howie?''

Howie stopped at the door and said, "Hard to say, when for some of us it's Halloween all year." He stepped down onto the sidewalk.

"What's the matter with Howie?" Danny said.

"He is uneasy in his skin," Elisa said.

Frankie merely shook his head as if to say it was too bad, and he understood, and he didn't know what to do about it.

Danny did not understand. Howie was having some kind of problem that had something to do with Halloween. Maybe he didn't have a costume. Maybe he was more upset by the fact that he didn't *need* a costume. Hoping to get some useful information, Danny said to Elisa, "Do you dress up for Halloween and go trick-or-treating?''

"Dressing up is usually not necessary," C.D. said as he straightened his bow tie, "but we try to fit in." He smiled, showing his two little fangs.

That didn't tell Danny much. He'd have to ask Howie about it later.

When Danny at last descended from the bus, he found the rest of the class gathered around Ms. Cosgrove, who was waiting near the ticket booth in front of the museum. Standing next to her was a tall, thin man who had hollow cheeks and a thin mustache over his pinched lips. His wispy hair was combed straight back and its tips touched his collar. He was dressed all in black, as if he were an undertaker.

"Class," said Ms. Cosgrove, "this is Mr. Price."

Mr. Price sounded like an announcer on a classical-music radio station. He told them how glad he was to see all of them and hoped they would have an educational experience. Again and again he reminded the students to be careful once they got inside the museum. Many of the wax figures were old, valuable, and could not be replaced.

Danny got the impression that Mr. Price did not really trust anybody with his waxworks. If he hadn't had to make a living, he probably wouldn't have let anybody inside.

The museum itself looked as if it had once been a movie theater. Faded posters promising marvels worth the price of admission hung inside glass cases that could have stood a washing.

"I am not familiar with this place," C. D. said as he shuffled with the crowd through the double doorway.

Danny said, "I've lived in Brooklyn all my life and *I've* never heard of it."

Inside, the place smelled like equal parts of ancient popcorn and modern chemical air freshener. Old couples carrying cameras over their shoulders on straps stood around the lobby studying the signs that were stuck on the walls everywhere. Each sign had a hand with a pointing finger drawn on it. The fingers pointed in different directions. One sign said THE MARCH OF HIS-TORY. Another said HURRAY FOR HOLLYWOOD. A third said INSPIRATION POINTS. There were also signs about famous lovers, famous scientists, and famous sports heroes.

Mr. Price led the class down a wide hallway covered with carpeting in a ghastly flowered pattern that reminded Danny of the covers on the furniture in his grandparents' house.

The hallway dimmed the further they walked, and soon they were walking past big, well-lit windows. Behind each was a scene from history. In one window, a bunch of guys in white wigs were signing the Declaration of Independence. Danny had to move around to get a better look through the tourists. In another window, Abraham Lincoln was giving his Gettysburg Address. His voice—or some actor's voice—crackled over a hidden loudspeaker.

There were other scenes. Some of them had sound and some did not. But in each one, full-size wax figures stood around as if they had just done something. Or as if they were about to do something. The comment he heard from the tourists over and over again was, "They look so real!"

Danny agreed. The more he studied the waxworks, the more they seemed just about to move. Even when the figures were good people like Eleanor Roosevelt or John Kennedy or Martin Luther King, Jr., the effect was pretty creepy. Suddenly, Danny was not looking forward to the Chamber of Horrors—full of guys who were not so nice.

Mr. Price stopped when he came to a black curtain. A sign over it said CHAMBER OF HORRORS—ABANDON

HOPE ALL YE WHO ENTER HERE. That's a cheery message, Danny thought.

When Ms. Cosgrove and the class had gathered around, Mr. Price told everyone how it was dark down in the Chamber, but that if you stayed on the lit path, you would be OK. "Please stay on the path," he said again, "and try not to faint." He made a thin smile then, and chuckled as if he had said something funny. To show how they weren't scared, the boys socked one another on the shoulder and reminded one another not to faint. Most of the girls tightly clutched one another's hands.

Elisa, Frankie, Howie, and C.D. looked interested in what they were about to see, but not in the least bit worried. This must be like old home week for them, Danny decided. One person's chamber of horrors was another person's family room. Howie leaned close to C.D. and said, "This can only give Stevie Brickwald ideas."

Elisa, who was standing on Howie's other side, said, "I believe that Stevie Brickwald is the least of your worries."

Howie snapped his head around to glare at Elisa. Danny thought for a moment that Howie was going to howl, but he only growled. Elisa smiled and said, "Remember who your friends are, Howie."

Howie said, "Quite," and nodded.

Mr. Price lifted one hand and dramatically thrust the black curtain aside. Beyond was darkness that seemed to be even more impenetrable than the curtain. "Follow me," Mr. Price said.

"Follow me," Ms. Cosgrove said, imitating Mr. Price's voice.

22

The class formed into single file to walk down the narrow stone stairs beyond the curtain. There was none of the pushing and shoving and wisecracking that usually accompanied this process.

Once through the narrow doorway, Danny saw that small, concealed lights were everywhere. He could actually see the stairs pretty well. The stairway twisted like a corkscrew down into the ground. The distance they'd come had to be an illusion. Who would dig a hole this deep just for a wax museum? The place began to smell damp. No one spoke. The only sounds were those of shoes against stones, air conditioning, and the breathing of the kids nearest him. Then, Danny heard creepy organ music.

The music got louder as they descended. Soon the stairway opened out into a huge cavern. Lighted alcoves occasionally punctuated the rough-hewn rock walls. Free-standing exhibits stood around the room under spotlights, each one surrounded by purple velvet ropes. One of the exhibits moved and Danny yipped. The rest of the class laughed. The exhibit that moved had really been a tourist. Danny could see that now.

Stevie Brickwald said, "I thought you'd be used to this stuff by now, Danny, considering the kids you hang out with."

"OK, kids," Ms. Cosgrove said, "spread out. But don't touch anything. And remember to stay on the lighted paths."

Gradually the class broke up. Danny walked off with Elisa and Frankie and Howie and C.D. The exhibits were interesting if gruesome. They saw Jack the Ripper threatening a London woman with a big knife. They saw

Anne Boleyn, Henry the VIII's second wife, about to be beheaded. They saw some poor woman about to be burned to death as a witch.

But the exhibits that caused the most comment among Danny's friends were the ones that had to do with classic monsters of history and legend. As it turned out, the creepy organ music was coming from one of these—an exhibit called "The Phantom of the Opera." Some guy with the ugliest face Danny had ever seen mechanically rocked up and back as he played a big pipe organ; a pretty girl cringed nearby. "Not a music lover, I guess," Danny said.

Next to the phantom was a mummy, awakened after three thousand years. He reminded Howie of his cousin, Anwar, from Egypt. After the mummy, they saw a guy in a tuxedo leaning over a pretty woman dressed all in white. C.D. laughed and said, "It looks like Uncle Fortesque."

In the alcove next to the vampire was Dr. Frankenstein bringing a monster to life. Frankie and Elisa studied the tableau critically. At last, Frankie said, "His wiring is not practical. His laboratory will blow up if he throws that switch." ·

When Howie saw the werewolf alcove, he just stood and stared. He did not say anything. He would not move on. He just stared. The exhibit showed a creature, half man, half wolf, standing across a room from a stooped old Gypsy woman. Drawn on the floor between them was a five-pointed star in a circle along with a bowl of fire and the letters from some strange alphabet. The plaque on the floor in front of the exhibit said that this old Gypsy woman was attempting to cure her son of being a werewolf by using spells and incantations.

"Pretty interesting, huh?" said Danny.

"Quite," said Howie. He just stood there staring.

"Let's look at something else," Danny said.

"You go ahead," said Howie.

Elisa dragged Danny away. Frankie and C.D. followed. Elisa said, "I think we are beginning to see Howie's problem."

"You believe he is upset about being a werewolf?" C.D. said.

Danny said, "He was busy memorizing that exhibit. Something must be going on."

They walked around the room, sampling the rest of the exhibits. They were all pretty much the same, people doing nasty things to one another. A little of this went a long way for Danny. He didn't even like to watch the news on TV.

In one alcove, a Dutch seaman was standing on the bridge of his schooner, staring out to sea through a telescope. "The Flying Dutchman," said C.D., reading the plaque. "Doomed to attempt forever to round the Cape of Good Hope."

"There's a button that says PUSH," Danny said.

Frankie pushed the button. In a moment the placid scene before them changed. Wind blew through the rigging. Rain fell. Lightning flashed. Thunder rumbled. And on the other side of the room, something howled in a way that made Danny's flesh crawl as none of the exhibits had.

"Howie," they all said together.

"It must be the storm," Frankie said.

25

Danny knew that Howie had a problem with thunderstorms. Apparently it made no difference if they were natural or artificial.

Howie ran around the room on all fours, howling again and again like a thing in pain. He was covered with hair. His ears were long, and his nose was flat. He ran through the crowd, scattering the shrieking kids and tourists while Ms. Cosgrove tried to regain control of her class. Some tourists thought Howie was part of the show till he ran into a guy being hanged. Howie knocked the guy's body loose and it fell to the floor while the head stayed in the noose.

"No!" cried Mr. Price as Howie continued to run around the room.

The tourists ran for the stairs and climbed over one another, trying to get away.

Howie ran through the torture chamber exhibit, got tangled in a rope with which some poor victim was tied to a rack, and pulled both arms from the statue's sockets. Howie continued circling the room, howling, pulling the bouncing arms after him, knocking things over.

It was not long before the storm in the Flying Dutchman exhibit automatically shut off. After that, Howie gradually calmed down, turned around three times, and went to sleep in a corner.

Mr. Price was in a rage. Shaking his fists and making wrathful noises, he confronted Ms. Cosgrove, but was so angry he could not speak.

"I'm sure we can pay for the damage," Ms. Cosgrove said. She looked around worriedly. "Somehow."

"Can you replace the *Mona Lisa*?" Mr. Price asked. "Can you replace Michelangelo's *David*?"

"Well," said Ms. Cosgrove, uncertain of how to answer.

Ms. Cosgrove gathered her students together. Howie woke up while all of them were watching Mr. Price wail anew every time he discovered more damage. Howie, not knowing how Mr. Price reacted to such things, offered to pay for what he had done. Mr. Price asked him about the *Mona Lisa* and the *David*. He sent everyone away. He would think of what to do and contact the school.

The students got back onto the bus, bubbling with excitement. For them, this was not the disaster it was for Mr. Price. Howie was very quiet. He and the other monster kids lagged back and boarded the bus just before Ms. Cosgrove.

"I'll talk to you back at school," she said as she shooed them aboard.

Danny was once more sitting next to Elisa, but he was watching Howie, wondering what was going through his mind. He did not have to wonder for long because Howie said something, obviously to himself but loud enough for those closest to him to hear. He said, "I don't want to be a werewolf anymore. It's nothing but trouble. I want to be a real boy."

"What?" C.D. leaned forward and whispered.

"I want to be a real boy. And I want to be one before Halloween."

Chapter Three

If Life Gives You Hair . . .

Howie did not say another word on the bus ride back to P.S. 13. When they were settled in the classroom, Ms. Cosgrove asked each of her students to write a report on their trip to the Price Wax Museum. She said, "I want to see reports on the museum, not on Howie." She looked so serious that nobody laughed. Not even Stevie Brickwald.

Danny couldn't think of what to say. He put down his pencil. He picked it up. A picture of Howie running around the Chamber of Horrors kept jamming his brain. Every time he looked up from his blank paper, he saw Ms. Cosgrove looking at Howie. She was probably trying to figure out what to say to him. Danny wanted to talk to Howie too and knew he would have the same problem.

Eventually, Danny got something down on the paper. He talked about the darkness and the smell and his reaction to all those people doing nasty stuff to one another. He didn't even mention the wolfman exhibit or the Flying Dutchman, let alone Howie.

A bell rang, marking the end of the school day. The kids looked expectantly at Ms. Cosgrove, but she was staring into the air, her mind a million miles away. Angela Marconi said, "Ms. Cosgrove?"

Ms. Cosgrove jumped as if Angela had awakened her from a deep sleep. She said, "Don't forget to study your spelling words. Class dismissed." The whole class pushed their chairs back but had not yet stood up when she went on, "Howie, can I talk to you for a minute?"

Howie didn't say anything. He just slunk over to Ms. Cosgrove's desk. The two of them stood there watching the other students leave. Danny went outside with Elisa, Frankie, and C.D. to wait for Howie in the corner made by the staircase and the building.

Barbara walked by with a bunch of her friends on her way to the Girls' Pathfinders meeting. They talked and laughed. Even Barbara seemed to be having a good time. Elisa waved at her and smiled hopefully. Barbara frowned and looked away quickly.

"Your sister does not like me," Elisa said.

"She doesn't know you very well," Danny said.

Elisa turned to watch the retreating fourth grade girls for a moment and then said, "I cannot wait for Howie. I must go to the Girls' Pathfinders meeting. Please tell him that I am his friend and that I will help him in any way that I can."

"He will certainly need it," C.D. said as Elisa followed the laughing group of girls.

Howie came out soon, staring at his feet as he dawdled down the stairs, scuffing the toes and heels of his running shoes.

"What did Ms. Cosgrove say?" Danny said.

"Not much," Howie said. "Just that I obviously needed professional help of some kind. She suggested either a psychiatrist or an allergy doctor. Perhaps both. I wish my problem could be solved so easily."

"What about Mr. Price?" Danny said.

"I am responsible for the damage. I'll take care of it somehow. We'll wait and see what Mr. Price says."

"Commendable attitude," C.D. said.

"Ms. Cosgrove said the same thing." He looked at Danny and went on, "I know you were supposed to come over this afternoon, but to be frank, I don't think I will be very good company. I have a lot on my mind."

"Perhaps we can guess what it is," said C.D.

"Look, chaps, you are all my friends, and I appreciate your concern, but I don't think there is anything you can do about my problem."

"We can't help being what we are," said C.D. "Besides, even being a werewolf must have its advantages. Find them. Use them."

"Sure," said Danny. "If life gives you hair, be a werewolf." He smiled, trying as hard as he could to make Howie smile with him.

Howie shook his head and said angrily, "Frankly, chaps, I don't see any advantages to running around like a wild animal and howling. Hair gets into everything. I cannot have a pet because animals are afraid of me. I cause a lot of trouble. My problem with Mr. Price was not the first incident of its kind."

"You are unyielding in this?" C.D. said.

"Absolutely. I want to be a real boy. And I want to be one soon. I do not wish to spend another Halloween as a werewolf."

Danny said, "Then you'll need a Gypsy woman like the one we saw at the wax museum."

Howie drew his thick eyebrows together as he considered this.

Frankie said, "Perhaps there is a better way. A more scientific way. My mother will be here soon. She will take us to my house. We will go down to the Mad Room and consult the data base."

"Ah, the data base," said C.D. and nodded.

"Worth a try," Howie said. And for the first time in days, Danny saw him smile.

The principal of P.S. 13 let the Girls' Pathfinders use a classroom for their meeting. Barbara stood next to Elisa Stein while they said the pledge of allegiance and the Girls' Pathfinders creed.

Across the circle, Barbara could see Laurie Perry standing next to Marcy Anderson. Laurie was tall and thin and Marcy was short and round. They looked funny together, as if they were the stars of a TV cartoon show. Barbara waved at Laurie, and she smiled and waved back. Barbara sighed.

Mrs. Bumpo explained the craft project of the day. She gestured with her glasses, which she held in one hand, and read from a three-ring binder, which she held in the other. The project was to make a garden of paper flowers, "because," Mrs. Bumpo said, "flowers are so pretty, and we miss them in the winter."

"I enjoy flowers," Elisa said.

"Sure," said Barbara. "Stepping on them or eating them?"

"Making them, perhaps?" Elisa said.

The Girls' Pathfinders sat in pairs, Big and Little Pals together, and, following Mrs. Bumpo's example, turned wire and colorful tissue paper and white glue into flowers. Laurie Perry and Marcy Anderson had made a whole bouquet while Barbara and Elisa were still working on their first flower. It's those monstery hands, Barbara thought. She can't do anything right.

"Look, it's coming apart," cried Barbara as one petal peeled back from another and showed gooey white glue.

"Too much glue," said Elisa.

"What do you know?"

Elisa sighed. "Very well," she said, "we make it dry faster." She held the wire stem of the flower in both hands and closed her eyes. Suddenly the wire glowed red, and the flower burst into flames. As surprised as anyone, Elisa dropped the flower on the floor and began to stomp on it to put it out.

Barbara shrieked and backed away. While Elisa danced on the flame, Barbara cried, "She tried to set me on fire! She tried to set me on fire!" The fire was soon out, and Elisa began to pick up the charred pieces while Mrs. Bumpo charged over to see what the problem was. The other girls gathered around.

Barbara hugged Laurie Perry tightly and wept into her shoulder. "She's a monster," Barbara wailed. "She tried to kill me! She wants to electrocute me and barbecue me and eat me and use my brain for science!"

"I am certain you are overreacting," Mrs. Bumpo said as she pulled Barbara away from Laurie Perry. She turned to Elisa and said, "How did the fire start?"

Barbara said, "She was holding the flower in her hand, and—"

"Please, Barbara. Well, Elisa?"

"We tried to dry the flower on the radiator. Stupid of me."

"Unwise, at the very least."

Through her sniffles Barbara asked if she could talk to Mrs. Bumpo alone. Mrs. Bumpo agreed, and the rest of the girls went back to their flowers while she and Barbara went out into the hallway.

"Well?" Mrs. Bumpo said as she perched her armless glasses on her nose.

Barbara said, "That Elisa is a monster. She set the flower on fire by holding it in her hands." Barbara didn't say anything about Elisa wanting her brain. Mrs. Bumpo didn't seem like the type to understand.

Mrs. Bumpo studied Barbara for a moment and then said, "Such stories will not avail you, Barbara. You might as well know that your mother has already spoken to me about Elisa Stein being your Big Pal."

"Well, then—"

"I will tell you the same thing I told her." Mrs. Bumpo folded her hands before her as if she were reciting. "In Life," she said, "we sometimes must deal with people who are less than perfect." She glared at Barbara. "Some of us are less than perfect, ourselves. Therefore, I believe that having a Big Pal who is not one's first choice is not only good training for Life, but also builds character. Do you understand, my dear?"

"Well, yeah, but—" Barbara's mind was a whirl of arguments she was sure would do nothing to change Mrs. Bumpo's mind. She almost said something about Elisa wanting her brain, but decided against it.

"Very well, then. I will also tell you this. Regardless of my feelings on the matter, there are no other Big Pals available. You will be paired with Elisa Stein or with no one." Mrs. Bumpo opened the door to the classroom and waved Barbara inside. Barbara felt angry, frustrated, and alone. Mrs. Bumpo was less than perfect herself, if you asked Barbara.

Barbara wanted to be a Girls' Pathfinder. She wanted to go on the overnight cookout. There was only one thing for her to do, and she was prepared to do it. She would tough it out. After Elisa murdered her in some terrible way, then everyone would be sorry.

Mrs. Stein was not much taller than Frankie, but her hair, piled high on her head, made her seem to tower over everybody. A chip of something that sparkled decorated each of the knobs on her neck. She drove a snappy arrow-shaped car that looked as if it belonged in the next century. It was red. Howie, C.D., and Danny used the telephone in the backseat to call their parents.

They arrived at the sprawling house at the top of Holler Hill Drive. The front of the house looked like a windmill. Frankie was about to lead his guests to the Mad Room when Mrs. Stein said, "I'll fix you boys a little snack."

"No pizza for me, please," C.D. said politely.

Mrs. Stein smiled and laughed. "I remember." She shook her finger under his nose teasingly. "I don't want you two turning into animals and running off again."

The last time Danny had been at the Stein home, Mrs. Stein had served pizza. The garlic in it had driven Howie and C.D. into a nervous frenzy and eventually transformed them. The incident had embarrassed everyone.

Howie, Danny, and C.D. followed Frankie down the hallway to the elevator. "Laboratory," Frankie called out to the elevator, and it took them down to an enormous stone room full of ancient scientific machinery—spark generators, grown-up-size tubes of bubbling water, control panels with huge dials and switches—surrounding a king-size marble slab. They walked through the room and down a sweeping stairway at its far end.

At the foot of the stairway was a room just as large as the one above, but this one was full of modern electronic equipment. An arcade's worth of video games was lined up against one wall. A complicated home entertainment center filled one big corner. Computers, printers, keyboards were everywhere. The whole room seemed to hum and vibrate with power. It seemed to be thinking.

Frankie sat down at one of the computers and said, "I will access the Intellectotron Database with my Rotwang Mark III. Intellectotron will tell us anything we want to know about werewolves."

"I'm game," said Howie.

Frankie brought up list after list of multiple-choice questions on his screen. Each time he made a selection, the screen changed and brought up another list.

"So this is a data base," C.D. said.

"I guess," said Danny.

Finally, Frankie stopped making choices and leaned back in his chair. "There it is," he said. At the top of the screen were the words LYCANTHROPY, ITS DESCRIPTION AND CURE.

Danny tried to sound out the first word.

Howie said it out loud easily. "Lycanthropy. The condition of being a werewolf."

"Wait," Frankie said. "I make you a hard copy." He pushed another key and a moment later page after page of print began to slide silently out of a box. "Laser jet printer," Frankie said proudly.

Howie read the pages as they came out of the printer. He said, "Most of this is just a history and description of werewolves." He picked up another page. "Hallo," he said excitedly. "This one says SOVEREIGN CURES." He read to himself for a few moments while his friends watched him and became increasingly curious.

"Well?" said Danny.

"Well," said Howie, "some of this is useful. I'm sure that the rest of it is superstitious nonsense." He set the stack of papers down. "The trick will be to tell which is which."

Chapter Four

The Hound of Heck

"Let's see," Howie said. "Garlic keeps werewolves away." He looked at his friends and laughed. "We know that works."

Danny nodded. It was good to see Howie feeling better. Danny knew that he himself always felt better if he was actually working on a problem, even if he did not yet have a solution. Howie was probably the same way.

"Stakes or silver bullets through the heart at the crossroads at midnight seem to be solutions that are much too permanent," Howie went on.

"It is unfortunate," C.D. said. "There are crossroads everywhere in Brooklyn."

"And the Lone Ranger used silver bullets," Danny said.

"He was a hunter of werewolves and vampires?" C.D. asked.

"He was a cowboy hero."

"Why, then, the silver bullets?"

"It's a long story," Danny said. "You can come over some time and I'll show you old TV episodes on videotape. My dad's been collecting them."

"Midnight is past my bedtime," Frankie said.

"It does not matter. Not one of us is the Lone Ranger. We have no silver bullets."

"Even if we had them," Howie said, "I'd rather you chaps didn't consider using them. There's no point my being a real boy if I'm not around to enjoy it. Eh, what?" He chuckled. "Let's see. One can take blood from a werewolf."

"Perhaps I can be of assistance," said C.D., showing his fangs when he smiled.

"I'll have to think about that one," said Howie, continuing to read as C.D. smacked his lips and drew his Thermos from inside his cape. He sucked on his Fluid of Life. Howie read, "Calling someone by name while he's in the form of a werewolf."

"We know that doesn't work," said Danny.

"Oh?" said Frankie and C.D. together.

"Sure. On that foggy night a few days ago Barbara and I ran into Howie in the park. I called him by name, and he stayed a wolfboy."

"Hmm," said Howie as he read the passage again. "Maybe it means that I should have called *you* by name while I was in wolf form."

"But you can't talk while you're in wolf form."

"So much for that wonderful idea," said Howie, reading on. "It says here that washing the werewolf in running water cures lycanthropy."

"Do you take showers or baths?" Frankie said.

"Baths, usually."

"Try a shower. The water is running."

"Maybe," said Danny, "it means running like in a stream or river."

"Not many streams in Brooklyn."

"And I don't fancy sitting in a gutter," said Howie.

"Take a shower," said Frankie again.

They all agreed that Howie taking a shower could not possibly hurt. But success seemed unlikely, even to Frankie.

"What is next?" said C.D.

"That's the lot," Howie said. He frowned as he shuffled through the sheets of paper looking for something he might have missed.

"It's a start," Danny said.

"There are still a few days till Halloween," said C.D.

Frankie nodded.

"Perhaps," Howie said, still considering. He went on, "Maybe there's a book at home that has the answer."

Danny thought about that. He said, "If your parents had a book that includes a cure for lycanthropy, wouldn't they have cured you already?"

"Possibly. But I'm not about to ask them about it. They may react as if I told them I wanted to cut off one of my arms. I think they actually *enjoy* being werewolves. Or they have gotten used to it, at least. No, I'll tackle the books first. My parents have a whole room full of them, of which I don't think they've read half."

"I'll come and help, if you want," Danny said.

"I, too," said C.D.

A moment later, Frankie said, "My English is not so good."

Howie said, "That's OK, Frankie. Your data base was a big help."

Frankie nodded and smiled with relief.

Danny and the others knew that Frankie was very

shy. His English was probably as good as C.D.'s, but he felt uncomfortable about meeting Howie's parents.

They decided that after school the next day, they would take the subway to Howie's house.

The next morning, Howie reported to his friends that he had taken a shower the night before, rather than a bath. He still felt no different. Though it was difficult to say for sure without seeing what effect a thunderstorm had on him, Howie suspected that running water was no more useful than name-calling as a cure for lycanthropy.

"Frankie and I have a fully equipped medical laboratory," Elisa said. "Perhaps the answer lies on the operating table."

Howie shivered. He said, "I appreciate the thought, but I feel my answer lies elsewhere. After all, as you know, there are some things people were not meant to tinker with."

Later, during arithmetic, a monitor from the main office brought Ms. Cosgrove a letter. Danny had never seen this happen before. Evidently, Ms. Cosgrove never had either, because she turned the envelope over and over in her hands while saying, "Well!"

"Who's it from?" Stevie Brickwald shouted.

"As a matter of fact, Stevie, it's from Mr. Price at the wax museum."

Howie groaned and put his head down on his desk.

"I'm sure it will be all right, Howie. We'll open it during recess. Just the two of us."

"Very thoughtful of you, Ms. Cosgrove."

Recess came. Danny and the others went outside and began to play handball. Danny actually won a round from Stevie Brickwald. Stevie was stunned by his loss and carried on, shouting and stamping his feet, claiming that Danny had cheated. But not one of the many witnesses would back him up. Still fuming, Stevie went to the end of the line.

When Danny saw Howie come out of the building, he purposely threw a game to Marla Willaby, who seemed delighted that her next opponent was Arthur Finster. Arthur had been her boyfriend since the previous morning, which, as far as Danny could tell, was some kind of a record.

Elisa, C.D., and Frankie drifted out of line and, along with Danny, joined Howie near the steps.

"Well," said Danny, "you're smiling, so the news can't be too bad."

"Not bad at all, if I do say so. Evidently, Mr. Price has found that the damage was not as severe as he had at first feared. He has been able to put just about everything back the way it was. The rack victim's arms were a little banged up, but Mr. Price believes that he can make the damage look like bruises. It's likely that a prisoner in a torture chamber would have them anyway."

"I am pleased," said Elisa.

Howie held up one hand. "Wait. You haven't heard the whole story. Since my, er, performance yesterday, all the tourists have come back and brought their friends. They all want to see the werewolf. Mr. Price has offered me a job."

"There you go," said Danny. "I'm a real boy and I could never get a job as a werewolf at a wax museum."

"I do not want his job. I do not wish to be a werewolf. Ask yourself this, Danny: Is the fun of playing

42

Long John Silver worth the trouble of having one leg cut off?''

"I am sure," said C.D., "that this argument makes sense to you, Howie. I, however, am confused."

Howie would not change his mind. He was pleased that Mr. Price was no longer angry with him. But Mr. Price's goodwill was not enough to make Howie satisfied with being a werewolf.

After school, the three boys took the subway to the Talbot Arms, the modern apartment building where Howie lived. C.D. particularly enjoyed the underground ride. It reminded him of home. "Though," he admitted, "home *is* more quiet."

The Talbot Arms was a huge white block rising thirty stories into the air. It looked as if it were made from sugar cubes. The three boys nodded to the uniformed doorman, walked through the quiet lobby, and got into the elevator. Howie pushed the top button, and the elevator took them to the penthouse. "We have the entire thirtieth floor," Howie said.

Once the elevator stopped, Howie had to push the floor buttons in a special order before the doors would open. When he saw what was beyond the doors, Danny cried, "Wow! It's huge!"

They stepped right into the living room. The entire place was paneled in wood. The furniture was wood with small needlepoint cushions at seats and backs. Big square paintings of hunting scenes covered the walls. All of them featured packs of dogs pulling down big animals. What wasn't wooden or painted or sewn was

43

brass that gleamed warm and yellow in the late afternoon sunshine.

Sitting on a long bench that served as a couch sat a very pretty woman who had billows of beautiful silvery hair flowing over her shoulders. This was Howie's mother, Mrs. Wolfner. She was reading *Astronomy* magazine, but she put it aside to meet Howie's friends. Danny liked her immediately, and so, it seemed, did C.D. After C.D. kissed her hand, he and Mrs. Wolfner began a conversation about the moon that C.D. was enjoying so much Howie had trouble dragging him away. Mrs. Wolfner even invited C.D. back to observe the moon from their rooftop observatory.

Howie took Danny and C.D. into the library and carefully shut the door. "Lotta books," Danny said as he gazed at them rising shelf after shelf to the ceiling. "Much information," said C.D.

Howie showed them the section on lycanthropy. It took up most of one wall. Some of the books were what Danny had heard called tomes—great ancient volumes whose leather covers were peeling and cracking. Others were more modern. There were even a few paperbacks, including one called *The World's Best Werewolf Jokes*. Danny read one and laughed.

"Something funny?" Howie said.

"Maybe," said Danny, suddenly embarrassed.

"Let's have it."

"OK." Danny read, " 'Son: "Mommy, mommy, I don't want to be a werewolf." Mother: "Shut up and comb your face." ' "

The joke was not very funny now. Nobody said anything for a while.

44

"Well, let's get started," said Howie as he pulled a book from the top shelf. It was *A Dog's Life*, and it was by some guy whose picture on the back cover showed him to be covered with hair.

Danny pulled down one book after another. In each one he looked for chapters, paragraphs, phrases having to do with a cure for being a werewolf. References were few. There were plenty of terrifying descriptions of werewolf hunts and what happened when the werewolf was caught. Despite this, Danny learned nothing useful that he didn't already know from old movies and from Frankie's data base.

C.D. seemed to be doing no better. He sucked on his Fluid of Life almost constantly, as if he needed it for comfort. He said to Howie, "Our people have similar troubles." Howie agreed.

Between the three of them, they took about an hour to check all the books on werewolves. Howie sat back in an enormous armchair and said, "Not a bloody thing."

C.D. looked up at him.

"Uh, sorry. You find anything, Danny?"

"Nothing we can use. It looks like the only sure cure for a werewolf is death."

Howie didn't say anything.

Danny said, "You know, there is one book we haven't tried yet."

Howie and C.D. looked at him without saying a word. They were curious but not hopeful.

Danny said, "The telephone book."

"I have one right here," said Howie as he pulled the Yellow Pages from a bottom drawer. "But I don't—"

"Let's see that," said Danny. He began flipping

through the pages, then ran his finger down a column. "No listing for Old Gypsy Women." He flipped some more pages. "No listing for Lycanthropy." Danny tried to find Werewolves, and then Metaphysical Cures. "Nothing," Danny said. He looked up and said, "What's Holistic Medicine?"

"No idea," said Howie.

"Hot Mud Therapy," Danny mumbled. He slammed the telephone book shut. "Nothing."

"I have a suggestion," C.D. said. "It is, how you say, a long bang."

"Long shot?" Danny said.

"Of course. It is this. In my neighborhood there are many small strange shops, many people recently arrived from the Old Country. It is possible that one of the people in these shops knows the old ways and could give us information not printed in books."

A smile spread across Howie's face. "That's wonderful!" he said.

Looking for old Gypsy women in C.D.'s neighborhood sounded like an all-day project. They would wait till the day after next, Saturday.

"Saturday is Halloween," Howie said.

"Not till the evening."

"Very well," Howie said. He shook hands with Danny and C.D.

After her bad experience with Elisa and Mrs. Bumpo, Barbara had managed to renew her enthusiasm for the Girls' Pathfinders. If there were a way to be in the club and yet have nothing to do with either her counselor or her Big Pal, she would find it.

Barbara wandered around the house looking for ways to win merit badges. Their beagle, Harryhausen, lying at her father's feet, gave her an idea. She went to ask Danny if she could borrow the nontoxic monster makeup kit he'd bought for Halloween. Though he hadn't yet used it himself, Danny agreed to what she had in mind. He figured that if Barbara were a successful Girls' Pathfinder, she might lighten up on Elisa.

They took Harryhausen into his room. While Danny held him and petted him to make him stay still, Barbara took the red crayon from the kit and began to draw dripping blood on Harryhausen's chin. Once he understood what Barbara had in mind, Harryhausen did not seem to mind much. He let her draw dark circles under his eyes and green splotches on his neck.

"There he is," Barbara said. "The Hound of Heck."

Danny looked at Harryhausen critically. "Definitely weird, but not very scary," he said. "Wait." Danny rummaged around in his closet for a moment and came up with a green rubber shrunken head he'd gotten at the circus. He tied it around Harryhausen's neck. "There," he said. "*Now* it's the Hound of Heck."

Barbara invited her father to come up and have a look at Harryhausen. "I made up Harryhausen for Halloween," she said. "Isn't that worth a theater arts merit badge?"

Mr. Keegan agreed that it was, and he signed the merit badge request form. Barbara waved the paper triumphantly in the air. When Mr. Keegan had gone back downstairs, she said, "I don't need that Elisa or anybody else."

"Elisa's not so bad," Danny said. "She would have been a big help with the Hound of Heck."

Barbara threw Danny a dirty look as she marched out of the room.

Chapter Five

Zelda Bella's Fruit

Barbara got up early on Saturday morning and began to tremble. Now that it came down to the crunch, she was afraid of going out to Long Island for the Girls' Pathfinders cookout.

The books she'd read itemized a number of terrible things that could happen to people out in the wilderness. There were broken legs, animal bites, and a strange and awful thing called "exposure." Which meant that just being out there could kill you.

Besides that, she couldn't tell from the line drawings and photographs in the books the difference between any of the plants. She could as easily step into poison ivy as into marsh grass. She couldn't tell the footprints of a mountain lion from those of a raccoon.

And even if she didn't get eaten by a wild animal or die of itching or drinking bad water, dumb old Elisa Stein could always drag her behind a tree and eat her and suck on her bones and carry her brain home in a plastic sandwich bag.

Still, Barbara didn't want to be the one to say she wouldn't go. She wanted somebody to forbid her. That way, one of her parents might sign her merit badge request form for the wilderness merit badge even if she never went. Just because they felt guilty.

But nobody would cooperate. Mrs. Keegan calmly reminded Barbara of how she had been looking forward to this and of what a good time she'd have. Danny got tired of the fuss pretty quickly. He said, "Besides, Elisa will probably bring a lunch. She won't want you till dessert."

"Danny!" Mrs. Keegan cried as Barbara shrieked and ran from the room. Danny said, "Elisa's OK, and Barbara probably knows it. Barbara just has this actress streak."

Danny was glad to get away from Barbara. He was meeting Howie at his house, and then they were picking up C.D. and the three of them were going to check out C.D.'s neighborhood for old Gypsy women.

After Danny left, Mrs. Keegan was able to quiet Barbara down and convince her that Long Island was not the middle of Borneo. The chances were very good that she would survive the experience. Barbara was not convinced. But after a while, she and her mom began to collect equipment that she would need for staying out overnight.

Howie was ready when Danny arrived at the Talbot Arms, and they didn't waste time as they crossed town to C.D.'s house behind the basement tailor shop the Bitesky family owned. As they walked from the subway, Howie kept stopping and looking into windows or sniffing at doorways. "This is positively capital! It was worth coming out here even if we never find an old Gypsy woman!"

Danny said "Yeah" as enthusiastically as he could, but he knew that the chances of some old woman in this neighborhood actually knowing how to cure lycanthropy were two: slim and none. And that if Howie went home still a werewolf, he would go home depressed, no matter what he said about it now.

While they waited for C.D. to come up from the catacombs below the tailor shop, Danny and Howie wandered up and down along the long hall in the Bitesky home, looking at the paintings of C.D.'s ancestors.

"There's something to be thankful for, anyway," Howie said. "At least we werewolves don't have a lot of old relatives hanging around."

C.D. showed up looking bright and fresh. It always amazed Danny that C.D. *didn't* look as if he'd slept in his clothes. But maybe he didn't. Maybe he wore pajamas to bed like everybody else.

"Where do we begin?" Howie said.

"Right outside the door," C.D. said.

The three boys walked up the stairs outside the Biteskys' Stitch in Time Tailoring Service and came to the sidewalk. C.D. led off. He pointed to apartment buildings where neighbors with strange names lived. They sounded strange to Danny, anyway, but C.D. had no trouble pronouncing them. The Straczynskis, the Blechmans, the Denizovitches. Some windows had construction paper cats or ghosts or jack-o'-lanterns taped to the windows, showing that there were children inside.

The boys stopped and each bought a bagel from a bearded old man who huddled into a long patched overcoat and carried his wares through their holes on a long stick. The bagels were fresh and miraculously still warm and cost only a quarter apiece. Danny had never tasted anything so good.

An enormous store called Moishe's Dance-and-Read had a loudspeaker out front that was blaring shrill, crazy music that made Danny want to dance. They looked inside and saw that half the store was taken up by bin after bin of record albums, many of them with labels written in some strange curvy letters. The other half of the store contained shelves of books, wall to wall, floor to ceiling, with aisles barely wide enough to allow a grown-up to pass. Cardboard boxes full of unsorted books stood in piles at the end of each aisle.

They passed a photographer's studio that had dark portraits of serious, old-fashioned European-type people in the window. Further on was a theater showing movies made in places like Latvia.

They spent a lot of time in a place called Cheapo City. It was a big store that sold nail clippers, plaster statues of Greek gods, pictures painted on velvet, underwear, kitchen gadgets, paper, pens—all kinds of interesting stuff, some of which neither Danny nor Howie had ever seen before. And it was all cheap. That was the great part. Danny wanted one of everything, and he could almost afford to buy it!

When they came out of Cheapo City, Danny had a new penknife. It didn't look very sturdy, but it had a skull and crossbones stamped on the side, and it had cost only fifty cents. "Where to next?" he said as he tried to open the blade without breaking it.

C.D. looked around, as if an old Gypsy woman had promised to meet them there and he wanted to be the first to spot her. "We go there!" he cried and pointed across the street.

Danny looked in the direction C.D. was pointing and saw a narrow shop, not much wider than its doorway. Its front was crossed with wide red stripes painted at an angle. Over the door was a sign that said ZELDA BELLA'S FRUIT in uneven hand-painted letters.

"Zelda Bella sounds like a Gypsy name to me," Howie said. He led the way to the corner, where the light seemed to take forever to change. But when it did, they crossed the street.

A bell tinkled when they opened the door and went into the cool, dim interior of the narrow shop. There was a powerful smell of fruit in the place. Flies circled in the air waiting for permission to land. Danny did not blame them for not setting down right away. The fruit in the wooden bins looked old and unhappy, as if it had been there for a while and somehow knew it would be there longer.

A woman came out from behind a faded red curtain holding a steaming coffee mug in one hand. The three boys studied her carefully. She was wearing a billowy blouse printed with white stars and a skirt that swept to the floor. A scarf was tied around her head, and a gold hoop earring dangled from one ear. Creases and folds covered her face. She seemed to be about a hundred years old.

"If she's not a Gypsy," Howie whispered to Danny and C.D., "she must be a pirate. That's almost as good."

"Help you boys?" the old Gypsy woman said. Danny could not yet tell whether she spoke with a foreign accent or not.

C.D. stepped forward and bowed. This seemed to astonish the woman for a moment. Then she gravely bowed back. C.D. said, "Excuse me, dear woman, but we are looking for a Gypsy."

"I sell fruit, boys. If you want Gypsies, try Cheapo City. They got everything else. Maybe they got that too." Danny was certain now. She didn't sound like the old Gypsy women in the movies. She sounded like some Brooklyn housewife.

"Are you Zelda Bella?" Danny said.

"Nobody else here, boy. Haven't got around to hiring my staff yet." She cackled crazily to herself for a moment. She stopped suddenly and said, "You boys want some fruit? Got some nice apples."

To Danny, the apples looked old, wrinkled, dusty, and tasteless. Zelda Bella didn't sprinkle her fruit with water the way the supermarkets did. Danny said, "No, thanks. Actually, we were looking for information." He prodded Howie with his elbow.

Howie glanced around the place, then said, "You see, we have a friend who is a werewolf, and we are looking for a Gypsy woman to cure him."

The flies buzzed for a while. Zelda Bella said, "Look, boys, I got no time for jokes. Either buy some fruit or get out."

"It is truth," said C.D.

Zelda Bella cocked her head and looked at them slyly for a moment. She said, "One of you boys a werewolf?"

Howie frowned.

"Maybe you," said Zelda Bella, "with all the hair and the pug nose."

"How'd you know?" Howie said.

"Just a guess. That 'my friend' stuff is older than I am."

"All right," said Howie. He stepped forward. Zelda Bella clutched her coffee cup and backed into the curtain. Howie stopped and said, "I am a werewolf, but I don't like it. It is beastly."

"Good word," Zelda Bella said.

"Quite. And I don't want to spend another Halloween that way."

Zelda Bella must have heard the desperation in Howie's voice because she took a sip of her coffee, bit her lip, and said, "All right, boys. Come into the back." Suddenly she was gone and the curtain was swaying gently.

"What do you think?" Howie said.

"We've come this far," Danny said.

C.D. agreed. The three of them walked to the end of the shop and crowded through the curtain. Beyond was a small room filled with furniture. It was all clunky old stuff with lace doilies on the arms and backrests. Each piece sat on its own blue flowered carpet. Hundreds of small framed photographs were arranged on the mantel over the fireplace. In a corner, a grandfather clock ticked away the seconds, announcing each one, making it sound important.

"Sit down, boys. Sit down." Zelda Bella waved them to a long couch that had clawed feet like an animal. From some room even further back she brought out a small brass plate and a glass of water and set them down on a low round coffee table in the center of the room. She lit a small green cone and blew it out and set it in the center of the plate. The cone glowed and the thread of smoke rising from it filled the room with a spicy, flowery odor.

With a grunt, Zelda Bella settled into a big armchair. "Let's see," she said and studied the glass of water. Howie, Danny, and C.D. leaned forward and looked into it too. Time passed, chopped off into neat bits by the ticking of the grandfather clock. Danny fidgeted. Zelda Bella grunted again and said, "Fruit is the answer."

"Fruit?" Howie said.

"Yes. You must rub the meat of three peaches all over your body. Three peaches"—she thought for a moment—"and three dog hairs."

"I have a beagle," Danny said.

"I know that," Zelda Bella said. "It was all in the water glass. It just so happens that beagles have the best hair for curing a werewolf."

"Are you certain of this?" Howie said suspiciously.

Zelda Bella shrugged and said, "If you don't believe me, get a second opinion."

"Perhaps we will," said Howie as he stood up. "It is not yet 11 A.M. We have plenty of time."

"The spell takes four or five hours to work. You don't have as much time as you think."

After thinking about that for a moment, Howie sat down.

C.D. said, "Where will we acquire peaches at this time of year?"

"I have some put away. I was gonna make jam out of them and never got around to it."

Howie said, "Excuse us," then walked back out into the store. C.D. and Danny followed. They discussed Zelda Bella's idea of a cure. None of them thought it sounded promising. Still, if they searched for another Gypsy to give them a second opinion, they might not have time to work Zelda Bella's spell before the sun went down. "We have no better ideas," C.D. said. "Even if it doesn't work, the fruit and dog hair will not harm you."

When they returned to the back room, Zelda Bella was writing something on a sheet of paper with a stubby pencil. "You'll need these magic words too," she said and handed the paper to Howie.

Howie read them and said, "Gibberish."

"I didn't say they'd be in English," Zelda Bella said.

She ended up charging them five dollars for three frozen peaches, the magic words, and the advice. "You have to supply your own beagle hair." She ushered them out the door, then locked it behind them and put up a CLOSED sign. Howie stood there with the other two, holding a brown paper bag in his hands.

C.D. said, "I have much to do before the sun goes down, so I cannot help you any further. But I hope that both of you will join my family and me in celebrating Halloween."

"I'll be a real boy by then," Howie said. "I'd be delighted."

"Me too," said Danny, while he wondered exactly how a family of vampires celebrated Halloween. He and Howie said goodby to C.D. and walked back to the subway that would take them to Danny's house.

Chapter Six

Dog Gone

Barbara stood in her bedroom, contemplating the official knapsack of the Girls' Pathfinders, which lay open on her bed. On top of the pile of clean underwear, vitamins, concentrated food sticks, matches, and other stuff she might need was her official pocketknife.

The pamphlet that came with the official Girls' Pathfinders knife said that it was good for whittling as well as for opening a cut through which she could suck out poison if she were bitten by a snake. Unless she were bitten in a place she couldn't reach. Then she would have to get somebody else to suck out the poison. In which case, she would probably die. It was too disgusting to even consider sucking poison out of somebody else, so she doubted that anybody else would do it for her. Yuck!

She'd waited all morning for somebody to forbid her to go on the cookout, but nobody had. Elisa and Mrs. Stein would arrive soon to take her away, and then it would be too late. She would have to go.

Barbara toyed with the notion that nobody loved her, that both her parents were in on some kind of plot with the Stein family, that somehow they would benefit from her not having a brain. The idea had a certain appeal, but Barbara could not convince even herself it was true.

Downstairs, Harryhausen began to bark, and Barbara ran to the window to see if Elisa and Mrs. Stein had pulled up. But there was nobody out there. Barbara sat down on her bed and began to look through the official *Girls' Pathfinders Survival Guide* again. She would stay in her room looking at it till somebody came upstairs to get her. Her exit would be more dramatic that way.

Danny played with his house key while he and Howie stood talking on the front steps of the Keegan home. Danny wanted him to come in and help cut three fresh hairs off Harryhausen, but Howie shook his head and said, "I'd better stay out here, Danny. I told you what happens to pets when I'm around."

"Harryhausen is a very friendly dog."

"That's not the point. Pets don't like werewolves. Turtles and goldfish don't mind so much. But dogs and cats go absolutely bonkers."

"Harryhausen isn't like that. You'll see." Danny opened the front door and shouted, "Mom, I'm home!" as he and Howie walked into the hallway. More quietly, Danny said, "Harryhausen should be around here some-place. Here, Harryhausen!"

Harryhausen ran out of a room at the other end of the hallway, lost his traction on the polished hardwood floor as he came around the corner, then yipped happily as he ran toward them. Suddenly, Harryhausen seemed to catch a whiff of something he didn't like, because he churned his feet backward, trying to stop as he contin-ued to slide forward on the smooth floor.

"Harryhausen!" Danny said with surprise.

Harryhausen skidded to a stop, his legs splayed out at odd angles, and barked a couple of times as he looked up at Howie. Howie shook his head and said, "You see? I told you," as Harryhausen backed off, growling.

"Harryhausen," Danny said again, but the dog continued to back off. "Come on, Howie."

"I don't know . . ." Howie said as Danny walked toward Harryhausen. Howie took a step. Harryhausen turned and ran.

"Come on," Danny cried and went after him.

"I'll wait here," Howie called to Danny.

Danny chased Harryhausen all around the house. Then, somewhere between the kitchen and the living room, Danny lost track of him. "Here, Harryhausen," Danny called, then stopped to listen.

Mrs. Keegan came into the living room with Howie and said, "Howie says that Harryhausen has run away."

"Away from us," Danny said. "Not away from home. At least I don't think so. At least I hope not. He's gotta be around here somewhere."

"What were you doing to the poor animal?" Mrs. Keegan said and began to look behind furniture.

"Nothing, Mom. We just came in and he took off like a shot." Danny glanced at Howie. Howie turned away and looked behind a chair. "Harryhausen?" he said.

"Very strange," Mrs. Keegan said. The doorbell rang. Mrs. Keegan said, "That'll be Elisa and her mother," then went to answer it.

Mrs. Keegan led Elisa and Mrs. Stein into the living room. Everybody made their greetings, and Mrs. Keegan went upstairs to get Barbara. Elisa said to Danny and Howie, "How are, er, things?"

"It's been a real interesting morning," Danny said. "And now my dog is missing!"

"I told him I shouldn't come in," Howie said.

Danny began to tell Elisa and Mrs. Stein all the places he'd looked for Harryhausen and felt himself going crazier by the minute. Harryhausen had never run away before. What if he thought Howie had come there to live! He might never come back. Werewolf cure or no werewolf cure, they had to find him!

A few minutes later, Barbara marched slowly downstairs followed by her mother. Barbara was dressed in her official denim Girls' Pathfinders camping outfit, and she was carrying her official Girls' Pathfinders knapsack. She felt as if she were going before a firing squad. She would refuse a cigarette, the way the heroes did in the movies. Though, she admitted, refusing a cigarette would be no big deal; she thought cigarettes were pretty disgusting anyway and would not have smoked one under any circumstances.

When they reached the living room, Mrs. Keegan said, "Say hello to Elisa, Barbara."

Fighting the urge to say "Hello to Elisa," Barbara just said, "Hello."

"Well," said Mrs. Stein, "we have a long ride ahead of us. Shall we begin?"

As Mrs. Keegan shepherded Barbara, who was still morose, out the door after Elisa and Mrs. Stein, Danny sat next to Howie on the couch trying to think of somewhere new to look for Harryhausen. He was in none of his usual hiding places.

Mrs. Keegan came back into the room and told them that if they needed more help looking for Harryhausen, she would be in the kitchen.

"Thanks, Mom," Danny said.

When Mrs. Keegan was gone, Danny turned to Howie and said, "Exactly how important is it for you to be a real boy by tonight?"

"It's very important," Howie said.

"Then I have to ask you a question. And I want you to think about it before you give me an answer."

"Quite," Howie said.

"How do you feel about using your werewolf senses to find Harryhausen?"

The expression on Howie's face did not change. But true to his word, he also did not say anything. "I'll be right back," Danny said.

He went into the kitchen and began to look in the floor-level cabinets. Mrs. Keegan cracked an egg on the side of a bowl and let the gooey stuff inside drop into whatever she was making. Without turning around, she said, "How could Harryhausen get in there? He can't open cabinets."

"I don't know, Mom. Harryhausen's a pretty smart dog."

But Harryhausen wasn't anywhere in the kitchen. Danny went back into the living room and sat down across from Howie. "Well?" Danny said.

"You're making me awfully uncomfortable."

"Look," said Danny, "we have to find Harryhausen. What if he got out somehow?"

"He'll come home by himself."

"Maybe. Haven't you ever seen any of those Disney

true-life adventures? All kinds of things happen to dogs who run away.''

"We'll find another dog."

"We're not just looking for a werewolf cure here, Howie. Harryhausen is my dog, and I want to find him.'' Danny felt himself getting angry. Here was this guy, a guy who said he was a friend, who wouldn't help him find his dog. It was un-American. Howie was English, of course. Maybe he didn't know these things. Or maybe Barbara had been right all this time. Maybe Howie wouldn't help because he was a monster.

Howie interrupted Danny's dire thoughts by saying, "I suppose you're right. Stiff upper lip, and all that. I'll do it.'' He stood up. "Where did you see Harryhausen last?"

"Thanks, Howie." Danny was really relieved. He didn't want to think he had been so wrong about a person. He said, "I saw Harryhausen right in here. Over by the doorway."

Howie walked to the doorway. He got down on his hands and knees and began to sniff the floor.

"Don't you have to transform?" Danny said.

"Actually, no. I just have to refocus my concentration. Like listening to something far away instead of close up." He crawled in a circle and at last said, "Ah, there he is." Howie followed the trail along the floor. It led to the front door.

"He *did* get outside!" Danny said, concerned.

"It would seem so."

Danny opened the door, and Howie slid outside. Danny watched him lean forward, leaving a trail of mist as he sniffed the cold sidewalk. Danny followed as Howie sniffed right across the grass and down to the curb. He sniffed up and down the curb for a while, ignoring Danny's demands to know what was going on.

At last Howie turned around and stood up straight. "I don't understand this," he said. "The trail just stops."

"But that's impossible," Danny cried.

"Impossible or not," Howie said, "Harryhausen came as far as this curb and vanished."

Chapter Seven

Roughing It

Danny had an urge to get down on his hands and knees and sniff around. Maybe he could find a clue that Howie had missed. Nobody was stopping him, of course, but he didn't have the sense of smell that Howie had, so all the sniffing in the world would be pointless.

Besides, Howie had probably not missed anything. Danny still felt guilty about thinking—even inside his own head—that Howie wasn't helping because he was a werewolf. Danny didn't want to make a mistake like that again.

He and Howie just stood there studying the blank curb.

All of a sudden, Danny knew what had happened. He began to jump up and down and shout, "I got it! I got it!"

"What? What?" Howie jumped up and down too, though he could not possibly know what was exciting Danny.

"This must be where Mrs. Stein parked her car. Harryhausen must have jumped into it to get away from you."

"How did he get the door open?" Howie said.

Same way he got the kitchen cabinets open, Danny thought. He knew that Howie wouldn't buy that any more than his mom had. He didn't buy it himself. A moment later, Danny said, "Maybe they left a door open while they loaded Barbara's stuff in the trunk."

"They will be back soon?" Howie said.

"No, no. They went to Long Island on a Girls' Pathfinders cookout. They won't be back till tomorrow night!"

"Well," said Howie glumly, "at least you know that Harryhausen is safe."

"Not necessarily," said Danny. "Harryhausen is a city dog. He could get hopelessly lost in the country. And besides, now we'll never be able to cure your lycanthropy before tonight."

Howie looked surprised for a moment, seemed to make a decision, then nodded. "Now what do we do?"

"We see if we can get my mom or dad to drive us to the Girls' Pathfinders camp on Long Island. I just hope Harryhausen hasn't gotten lost already."

They found Mr. Keegan in the garage painting a chair blue and explained to him what had happened. All except the part about Howie being a werewolf.

"If Harryhausen is with Barbara and the rest of the Girls' Pathfinders, he'll be OK till tomorrow night."

"I don't know, Dad," said Danny. "He could get eaten by a bear or something." He was beginning to get really upset.

"Now you're starting to sound like Barbara. Do you like this color?" He studied his freshly painted chair critically.

"It's OK. But look, Dad, even if Harryhausen doesn't get eaten by a bear, I'll bet he'll be a lot of extra trouble

67

for somebody. And you know Barbara. It won't be her."

Mr. Keegan looked from the chair to Danny, then glanced at Howie. Howie smiled broadly and gave him the thumbs-up sign. "Please, Dad," Danny said. He hated to plead, but there was a time for everything.

"All right," Mr. Keegan said. "Let me change out of these painty clothes." He went into the house and the two boys shook hands.

Barbara had heard about Hell. It wasn't just a bad word. Some people said that it was a real place where mean people went when they died. Well, Barbara felt that she was there now. And she was only in the fourth grade.

The main difference between Hell and where she actually was, as far as Barbara could tell, was that Hell was hot and full of devils while the Girls' Pathfinders cabin was cold and full of dirt. Even the fire in the fireplace at one end of the room seemed to heat only the fireplace.

Heat was only in the fireplace, but dirt was everywhere. You could track it in from the Great Outdoors without half trying. There was grit in her hair, in her clothes, in her bunk. And she had to share everything, even the bathroom, with the other girls. Of course, she had to share a bathroom at home too, but at home, only one person used it at a time.

Though Barbara and Elisa and Mrs. Stein had just arrived at the camp, Barbara felt as if she'd been there for years. She sat on the edge of her bunk next to her knapsack, which was still packed, contemplating the long, cold, gritty, boring weekend ahead. Was she really cut out to be a Girls' Pathfinder? While she thought about this, she looked right through Mrs. Bumpo and Mrs. Stein and all the girls who were gathered at a table near the fireplace, studying the leaves and pinecones they had collected.

Mrs. Bumpo had a hearty attitude toward everything. Each new insult, each new hardship was seen by her as a challenge to be enjoyed and overcome. "You're soft from city living, girls. Enjoy getting in touch with nature." She would inhale deeply and exhale a plume of frosty breath.

Sure. With all that extra blubber on her, Mrs. Bumpo probably wasn't bothered by the cold. Barbara decided that next time she wanted to get in touch with nature, she would call it long distance. If she hadn't so desperately wanted her wilderness merit badge, Barbara would already have asked to be taken home. She sighed. Mrs. Bumpo had made it clear that deserters did not win merit badges.

"Barbara?"

Barbara looked up to see Elisa standing there, smiling down at her. Elisa said, "We are going out for more dogwood leaves for our autumn mosaic. Would you like to come?"

Barbara knew that it was colder and dirtier outside than it was in the cabin. Still, if she was going to win her merit badge—

"Or," said Mrs. Stein as she joined Elisa, "would you rather sit here and mope?"

"I don't know," Barbara said. The monsters were ganging up on her. Why didn't they leave her alone?

Mrs. Stein said, "Mrs. Bumpo has already noticed you in a way I do not think you wish to be noticed. Perhaps if you come with us, she will change her low opinion of you."

"Besides, an expedition will be fun," Elisa said.

"All right," Barbara said. It might be fun. It would be different, anyway. She put her official Girls' Pathfinders pocketknife in her pocket and slung her official Girls' Pathfinders flashlight in a special loop on her belt. Ready for anything, Barbara followed Elisa and Mrs. Stein to the front of the room.

Mrs. Bumpo glared at Barbara as she joined the six girls who were waiting at the door. Barbara experimented with a weak smile, but earned only a curt nod from Mrs. Bumpo.

A moment later they were outside, walking across the open space, strewn with brown pine needles, where the cars were parked. There was no wind, no sound at all, just a great waiting silence. The world seemed encased in cold crystal. Suddenly, something yipped like a small dog. It was not far away. Forgetting who she was with, Barbara grabbed Elisa's arm and cried, "What was that?"

"Probably a fox," Elisa said. She patted Barbara's hand. Embarrassed, Barbara pulled her hand away.

From even closer there came more barking. But these barks were oddly muffled and were soon joined by frantic muffled scraping noises. "What's that?" Barbara said.

"I don't know," Elisa said.

The noise seemed very close indeed, and a moment later, Mrs. Bumpo was standing next to the futuristic Stein automobile demanding to know, "What is the meaning of this?"

"That's Harryhausen!" Barbara cried. She saw him inside the Stein automobile, jumping up and down and barking and pawing energetically at the closed window. He got even more excited when he saw Barbara.

Mrs. Stein unlocked the door, and Harryhausen leaped out into Barbara's arms. He madly licked her face until she dropped him, and then he ran around in circles just as madly, barking happily.

"What is that animal doing here?" Mrs. Bumpo demanded.

"That's Harryhausen, my brother's dog."

"I didn't ask whose dog it was. What is it doing here?"

Neither Barbara, nor Elisa, nor even Mrs. Stein knew for sure the answer to that question. Elisa said, "Perhaps he jumped into the car when we picked up Barbara at her home and fell asleep under a pile of supplies."

"He always takes naps in the car," Barbara added, nodding.

Mrs. Bumpo pointed at Barbara and said, "In any case, now that he is here, you are responsible for him."

"Yes, Mrs. Bumpo."

Mrs. Bumpo sniffed haughtily, as if Barbara had unaccountably disagreed with her, then marched off along a path into the forest. The girls followed. Harryhausen scampered happily at Barbara's feet. It was good to see old Harryhausen again. Barbara didn't feel

quite so lonely or put upon with this little bit of home nearby.

The path wound through landscape that was stark and beautiful. Maples, dogwoods, and oaks raised empty branches to the sky. The ground was covered with colorful leaves, as if the trees had thrown a rowdy party the night before and no one had bothered to sweep up the confetti. As the Girls' Pathfinders walked, Mrs. Bumpo lectured on the wonders of Nature. Once, she pointed out rabbit tracks in a patch of mud. Almost against her will, Barbara found this exciting. Real rabbits!

Harryhausen seemed to be having a good time. Over and over again, he sniffed along the ground, following some scent for a few paces, then bounded back to Barbara to tell her all about it.

"Please keep that dog quiet," Mrs. Bumpo said more than once. "He's scaring all the animals."

"Someone should tell her that a dog is also an animal," Elisa said to Barbara.

This astonished Barbara, for she had been thinking exactly the same thing. Could Elisa read her mind? The prospect was frightening. Worse, Elisa would know that Barbara found the prospect frightening. Barbara looked at Elisa. But Elisa was not looking at her. She and her mother were studying a clump of moss growing on a tree.

Barbara watched as Harryhausen once again picked up an interesting scent and followed it into the forest. She assumed that he would come back in a second or two as he had so many times before, but this time he did not. He followed the scent up a ridge.

"Harryhausen," Barbara called, "come back." She

knew her brother would kill her if anything happened to that stupid dog.

Harryhausen stopped at the top of the ridge, barked a few times, then ran out of sight down the other side. Barbara ran after the dog, calling his name.

Mrs. Bumpo called after her, "Where do you think you are going, young lady?"

Barbara stopped and looked back at Mrs. Bumpo. She said, "I'm going after Harryhausen. You said I was responsible for him."

"Very well, but remember that *I* am responsible for *you*. Do not get lost."

"Yes, Mrs. Bumpo." Barbara ran up the ridge. She soon came to the top and could see Harryhausen below, nosing around a fallen tree. A moment later, Elisa ran up behind her and said, "I told Mrs. Bumpo that I would help you."

"Oh, you don't have to do that," Barbara said in what she hoped would be a convincingly concerned way. She had enough to worry about without having to worry that some monster was going to eat her brain. This would be a perfect opportunity for Elisa to do that—when they were off by themselves. Elisa could say that Barbara had had an accident.

"I am your Big Pal. And I want to be your friend."

Elisa seemed so sincere that Barbara could say nothing but "Thanks."

Barbara looked down at the fallen tree but could not see Harryhausen. "Come on," Barbara said and ran down to where the fallen tree was. She and Elisa climbed the horizontal trunk and stood atop it looking around.

"Harryhausen!" Barbara shouted. She heard barking far away.

"That way," Elisa said and pointed.

They ran as fast as they could in the direction of the barking. Leaves flew around them, raising a spicy odor. Bare bushes scratched at their pants legs. Once, they had to cross a stream on big smooth stones. Barbara almost fell into the icy water, but Elisa held her firmly by the arm. Barbara wondered when Elisa would make her monster move.

Later, they stopped and leaned against a big boulder. They had not seen Harryhausen for a long time. It had even been a long time since they'd heard him bark. "Maybe a bear ate him," Barbara said.

"According to the *Girls' Pathfinders Survival Guide,* the biggest animal out here is the fox."

"Harryhausen is a city dog. He's soft from city living just like we are. He wouldn't be much of a match for a fox who lives out here."

"Still, the fox does not know that."

That was true. Barbara felt a little better. "Harryhausen!" she called for the millionth time.

Very soon she and Elisa heard something moving noisily through the undergrowth. They stopped to listen. "If we can hear it, it can't be a forest creature," Barbara said, hoping it was true. "Harryhausen?" she said in a shaky voice.

Seconds later, Harryhausen scampered out from around the boulder they were resting against. He ran up to Barbara and Elisa to say hello as if he had been away only a moment. They both got on their knees to pet him and scratch him behind the ears. It was a happy reunion.

Elisa stood up and said, "We had better get back. Mrs. Bumpo will be worried about us."

Barbara stood up too. Harryhausen sat between them, his tail thumping on the ground. "Uh, which way?" Barbara said.

Elisa looked around and said, "I don't know."

Barbara felt a coldness that had nothing to do with the temperature of the air. She walked a few feet one way, then the other, hoping something would look familiar.

Elisa said, "I think, perhaps, we are as lost as Harryhausen."

Barbara had to agree. She recognized nothing.

Chapter Eight

The Call of the Wild

Howie and Danny didn't say much on the drive out into the wilds of Long Island. They were on a serious mission, and that seemed to call for everybody to act grown-up. Even if they'd felt like talking, however, they would have had a difficult time getting a word in edgewise around Mr. Keegan.

He began by lecturing Danny on responsibility. But after a while, Mr. Keegan distracted himself with memories of the summer camp he used to go to when he was a kid. Danny liked these stories but didn't believe much about them. For one thing, it was hard to believe that his father had ever been a kid.

Danny thought a lot about Harryhausen. He really loved that dog. He hoped that Harryhausen was doing OK out in the wilds. He was a dog who had no more experience in the wilds than Barbara.

Howie kept looking at his watch. If Zelda Bella was right about how long it took for her spell to work, Howie did not have much time to become a real boy before Halloween really began in earnest that evening. Danny himself was not certain that the spell would work at all, not even if they gave it years.

Following the signs, they soon turned off the main highway and drove onto a gravel road. After a few miles, they left the gravel road for a rutted dirt trail that cut through a beautiful woods. Mr. Keegan drove slowly, but his big car was not really an off-road vehicle, and it bounced them around a good deal. Howie hung out a window, with his nose high in the air. He was smiling. "Smells great," he said.

Soon the trail ended at the Girls' Pathfinders cabin. Mr. Keegan had Danny knock on the door, though that seemed a little silly out here in the wilderness. The door was answered by Mrs. Stein, who, with some surprise, said, "Danny!"

"Hi, Mrs. Stein. We're here to pick up Harryhausen."

"That is impossible at the moment, I am afraid."

"Huh?"

She invited Danny and Howie and Mr. Keegan into the cabin. Mrs. Bumpo was leaning over a map she had spread out on the table near the fire. Girls were watching intently as she pointed out landmarks with a pudgy finger.

Mrs. Bumpo fixed Danny and Howie and Mr. Keegan with a steely gaze and said, "Boys are not permitted at Girls' Pathfinders Camp." Howie and Danny shuffled uncomfortably. Even Mr. Keegan seemed to shrink a bit.

"We're just here to pick up Harryhausen," Howie said.

Mrs. Stein explained how Barbara and Elisa had gone after Harryhausen and how they were now all lost in the woods. She nodded at Mrs. Bumpo and said, "We were just about to send out a search party." Mrs. Stein seemed pretty upset.

"We'll look too," Danny said. Howie agreed.

"This is not a boys' camp," Mrs. Bumpo said again, as if that were a reason for Danny and Howie not to help.

"How can that possibly matter?" Mr. Keegan said. He studied the map for a moment, and then said, "You know, I learned all about rugged terrain when I was in the Boy Trailblazers—"

Mrs. Bumpo sniffed contemptuously.

"—and I'd like to help you with the search too."

"Thank you," Mrs. Stein said.

"I refuse to be responsible for more lost children," Mrs. Bumpo said. She glared at Mr. Keegan. "Or adults."

"We won't get lost," Howie said. "Back in England, I, too, was a member of the Boy Trailblazers. I have a merit badge in woodcraft."

"Most impressive, I'm sure," said Mrs. Bumpo, who did not sound impressed at all. But she made no more objections.

Danny could see that Mrs. Bumpo was having trouble deciding whether she should go out searching or if she should stay at the cabin and plan strategy. She watched Mr. Keegan as he pointed out things on the map to the girls. "There's a river. And look, a hill." He seemed very pleased with himself. Maybe all that stuff about summer camp was true, even if Mr. Keegan had never really been a kid.

At last, Mrs. Bumpo decided that going was better than staying. She warned them once more ("I am not responsible''), but she did not insist on having her way, so Danny and Howie went out searching with her and Mrs. Stein. They walked along the path until they came to the place where Barbara and Elisa and Harryhausen had left it.

Mrs. Bumpo said, "You will go that way. Mrs. Stein and I will go this. I hope, Master Wolfner, that your merit badge was earned. We do not wish to have to find anyone else. Come along, Mrs. Stein." She stepped off, a one-woman parade, with Mrs. Stein close behind.

More slowly, Danny and Howie searched in the other direction. "Cold," Danny said. Howie nodded. As they walked, Danny swept his eyes along the ground, looking for anything to indicate the two girls or the dog had passed that way. Every so often, Howie would stop to pile up some rocks to mark their own trail.

"It all looks the same to me," Danny said as he surveyed the rocky ground around them.

Howie said "Me too, actually."

"What about that merit badge?"

Howie scratched his head as he glanced around. "It's amazing how fast that woodcraft knowledge leaks away when you don't use it."

"We could stumble around here for days."

"Indeed," Howie said. "But I have an idea."

"What?"

"If I become a wolfboy, I can track them by scent and hearing and instinct."

"You didn't have to transform when you tracked Harryhausen back at the house."

"No. But here we have a much wider area to cover. The problem is much more complex."

Danny knew that ever since the incident at the wax museum, Howie had wanted nothing so much as to stop being a werewolf. Yet here he was, volunteering to go into werewolf mode. This was a Big Deal. "You sure?" Danny said.

"Do you think Mrs. Bumpo and Elisa's mother will have more luck than we are having?"

"I doubt it."

"Well, then, it's the only way."

"It's OK with me if it's OK with you. But can you do it without a thunderstorm?"

"It's just a matter of letting go," Howie said as he backed away from Danny.

Danny watched Howie, fascinated.

Barbara and Elisa stumbled along in silence. They were too tired to talk. Barbara had never felt so bone weary. Even her brain seemed to be dead, though Elisa had not touched it. Harryhausen had lost interest in exploring the woods and kept close to them.

Shadows were lengthening, filling the spaces between the trees with darkness. Pretty soon, Barbara pulled out her official Girls' Pathfinders flashlight and turned it on the ground before them. They kept walking until they came to an open place that during the summer may have been a good place for a picnic. Now, at the ragged end of fall, it just looked dismal.

Barbara poked her flashlight beam around and said, "I think we've been here before."

"Perhaps," Elisa said. She sounded brain dead too.

"Look at this," Barbara said. She had found an old dead tree that looked as if once, a long time before, it had been blasted by lightning. It was hollow, and there was just enough room inside for all three of them. They discussed staying there till morning so that they didn't get more lost than they were. "I think staying in one place is a good idea," Elisa said.

They settled in with Harryhausen between them and watched the woods get darker. Elisa put her arm around Barbara. Barbara stiffened under her touch, then relaxed as she noticed how comforting it felt to have somebody warm close to her. Somewhere, zillions of crows cawed to each other till they settled down for the night. Pretty soon, the two girls couldn't see anything. That was OK for a while, then they began to hear the wind in the trees and night animals moving around.

Barbara said, "I'm scared," then turned on her flashlight. The light seemed very bright. They found a little pocket of nuts in the tree with them that must have been forgotten by some squirrel. "Should we eat them?" Elisa said.

"I don't know. All the nuts I ever ate came in a can or a plastic bag."

They didn't eat the nuts, but they did leave the flashlight on, more for comfort than because they needed it to see. After a while, the light began to fade. It got yellower, then browner, then went out all together. "Dead batteries," Barbara said.

Elisa took the flashlight and opened it up. She held the batteries between the palms of her hands. Little sparks flickered between the battery terminals and Elisa's palms.

"Wow," said Barbara, "you really are full of electricity." Oddly enough, though Barbara was fascinated by what Elisa was doing, she wasn't frightened.

Elisa put the batteries back into the flashlight and turned it on. The light blazed as it hadn't for hours. "Thanks," Barbara said.

"My pleasure," Elisa said.

Barbara had once told Danny that his weird friends gave her the Flying Wallendas. It occurred to her that Elisa had not given her the Flying Wallendas for a long time. The truth was, Elisa did not seem to be a very frightening person. Maybe she never had been. Barbara thought about that. At last she said, "Elisa, I'm sorry I've been such a creep."

"I am sorry that it took us so long to be friends."

"Yeah." Barbara looked out into the unfriendly darkness, tried to make sense out of the rustlings and whistlings and barkings the cold wind brought her. "But I don't think I'll ever get used to nature. Maybe I can get a merit badge for gardening or auto mechanics or something."

Far away, something howled and chilled Barbara. Harryhausen growled, then began to whimper. Barbara scratched him between the ears while she said, "Sounds like one of your friends."

"Perhaps. But we are a long way from Brooklyn. I suggest we turn off the flashlight."

Barbara agreed, and it was done. A few minutes later, the call came again, this time much closer. Barbara and Elisa squeezed together more tightly. Harryhausen, who was between them, did not protest.

Then something came crashing through the foliage. "Stay here," said Elisa as she climbed out of the tree.

Barbara's eyes had gotten used to the darkness. She could see Elisa standing before the tree, her fists out, ready to electrocute anything that attacked. The howl came again, and a hairy creature broke from the bushes. Elisa opened her hands and shot lightning at the thing, shoving it onto the ground.

A second creature stumbled from the bushes and Elisa held up her hand to fire again when the thing shouted, "Elisa! It's me, Danny!"

Barbara and Harryhausen leaped from the hollow tree. Barbara threw her arms around Danny and cried. Elisa slapped Danny on the back. Harryhausen barked and barked but kept his distance. The thing that Elisa had zapped lay as if dead.

But Howie wasn't dead. The lightning had surprised him but hadn't hurt him much. Wolfboys are pretty tough. As he usually did after changing from wolfboy back to human, Howie had been taking a little nap, that was all.

When he awoke, Elisa apologized to him. Howie told her not to worry, that maybe she had jolted loose an idea in his brain.

Though he managed to lead them unerringly back to the Girls' Pathfinders cabin, Howie was quiet, as if he had something on his mind. Harryhausen trotted way off to one side, staying as far away from Howie as he could.

As she tramped through the darkness, now not afraid of anything, Barbara talked about how brave Elisa had been, climbing out of the tree to face the terrible animal

that had been attacking them. The fact that the animal had turned out to be Howie didn't matter. At the time, Elisa hadn't know what it was.

Elisa modestly turned the conversation to how lucky it was that Howie was a werewolf and how he could never have found them if he hadn't been one. Barbara and Danny agreed, though Danny with less enthusiasm. Danny knew what Howie was thinking about.

By the time they returned to the Girls' Pathfinders cabin, Mrs. Bumpo and Mrs. Stein were already there, huddling over the map with Mr. Keegan. They were planning a new strategy. Mrs. Bumpo looked a little miffed that further searching was not necessary. Elisa and Mrs. Stein had a reunion that Danny thought was a little stiff, but they seemed happy to see each other.

Mrs. Bumpo said, "You have your dog, Mr. Keegan. I'll thank you to take it and your son and his friend and leave. Our cookout has already been disrupted enough."

"I want to go home too," Barbara said.

"I also," said Elisa.

Mrs. Bumpo said, "I suggest you both stay. There will be no further chances to earn your woodcraft merit badges till next summer."

"I'll live," Barbara said, shocking Mrs. Bumpo.

Mrs. Bumpo stood around, looking as if she had been betrayed, while Barbara and Elisa packed. Barbara wanted to ride back with Elisa and Mrs. Stein. "We're going to talk about stuff boys wouldn't understand," Barbara said. She and Elisa clutched at each other and laughed.

"I think Harryhausen will want to go with you," Danny said to his sister. The dog was still giving Howie a wide berth. "After all, you found him," he added generously.

Later, Howie sat next to Danny on the front seat as Mr. Keegan drove them back to Brooklyn. Howie and Danny talked about what had happened in the woods.

"But," said Mr. Keegan, "I still don't understand how you happened to come across them in the dark."

"I owe it all to the Boy Trailblazers," said Howie.

Back in Brooklyn, Mrs. Stein pulled up right behind Mr. Keegan. It was much earlier than Barbara or Elisa or Danny or Howie imagined. The darkness and excitement had thrown them off. There was still plenty of time to get to C.D. Bitesky's Halloween party and maybe even to go trick-or-treating.

As they got out of the car, Danny pulled Howie aside and said, "We have an entire dog full of hairs now. You want to try Zelda Bella's spell?"

"I'm not sure," Howie said. "Look, I'm going home. I'll see you later at C.D.'s party."

"You sure?"

"For now, anyway."

Elisa was going to the party too. Barbara said, "I'm not afraid of anything when I'm with my friend Elisa. I'd like to go with her."

Elisa nodded, and Danny called C.D. to ask him if it was all right.

"I would be charmed," C.D. said.

When she heard his answer, Barbara said, "Just don't let him kiss my hand."

Elisa and Mrs. Stein left, saying they would be back soon with Frankie to pick up Barbara and Danny.

Long before Halloween, Danny had decided on a costume he hoped would not offend anyone or make his new friends uncomfortable. He had taken a bunch of paper bags and tied and taped them all over himself. He told everybody that he was a giant robot that could fold up into a one-person star ship.

Barbara was dressed up as a Gypsy fortune-teller. Danny was afraid of how Howie might feel about this, considering Zelda Bella and all, but he couldn't think of a way to persuade her to change her costume without telling more of the truth than he cared to.

Barbara and Danny climbed into the backseat of Mrs. Stein's car. Two very strange creatures were already sitting back there. "Hi!" said Frankie's voice. It came from a kind of lizardy creature with the head of an angry fish. "I'm the Creature from the Black Lagoon."

"And I," said Elisa, "am a Valkyrie. I carry heroes killed in battle off to their heavenly reward in Valhalla." She shook a rake at them and told them it was supposed to be a spear. She wore a helmet with two big wings on it, and a lot of cardboard armor.

They arrived at the Biteskys' Stitch in Time Tailoring Service. The four kids clattered downstairs, uncertain of their footing because of masks and outsized funny shoes.

C.D. met them at the door. He looked really strange because half of his face was normal, but the other half of it was made up to look angry and awful. "Allow me to introduce myself," he said. "I am both Dr. Jekyll *and* Mr. Hyde."

They walked through the tailor shop and into the Biteskys' private quarters. The walls and ceiling were hung with orange and black crepe paper. Jack-o'-lanterns

sat on every table and on either end of the fireplace mantel. No jack-o'-lantern was without its dish of candy or fruit. There was a big washtub full of water and apples for dunking. Standing at the fireplace sipping with difficulty from a mug of apple cider was a figure wrapped in gauze and tape.

"I came as Cousin Anwar," the mummy said. It was Howie! There was a difficult moment when he saw Barbara in her Gypsy costume, but he only smiled and said, "Capital! I want you to tell my fortune." He held out his hand to her.

Barbara took it and studied it carefully. Everybody laughed and made comments. When Barbara ran her finger over Howie's palm, she found that it was covered with soft fuzz, like a peach. In a mysterious voice, she said, "I see that you are a werewolf."

The joking stopped suddenly. Leave it to Barbara, Danny thought, to embarrass everybody. Every face that was not hidden by a mask looked serious. They all waited to see what Howie would say.

Danny was surprised when Howie laughed and said, "And I'm going to stay that way. If I weren't a were-wolf, some of my best friends would not be here tonight!"

Barbara said, "Hey, who's the fortune-teller around here?"

"I am," said Mrs. Bitesky from the doorway. She was dressed like a Gypsy too, and carrying a big tray. "And I predict that each of you will want one of these candy apples."

It turned out that she was right.

MEL GILDEN is the author of the acclaimed *The Return of Captain Conquer*, published by Houghton Mifflin in 1986. His second novel, *Harry Newberry Says His Mom Is a Superhero*, will be published soon by Henry Holt and Company. Previous to these novels, Gilden had short stories published in such places as *Twilight Zone—The Magazine*, *The Magazine of Fantasy and Science Fiction*, and many original and reprint anthologies. He is also the author of the first hair-raising Avon Camelot adventure of Danny Keegan and his fifth grade monster friends, *M Is For Monster*.

JOHN PIERARD is a freelance illustrator living in Manhattan. He is best known for his science fiction illustrations for *Isaac Asimov's Science Fiction Magazine*, *Distant Stars*, and SPI games such as Universe. He is co-illustrator of Time Machine #4: *Sail With Pirates* and Time Traveler #3: *The First Settlers*, and is illustrator of Time Machine #11: *Mission to World War II*, Time Machine #15: *Flame of the Inquisition*, and most recently *M Is For Monster*.